Agatha

Girl of Mystery

GROSSET & DUNLAP
Published by the Penguin Group
Penguin Group (USA) LLC, 375 Hudson Street, New York, New York 10014, USA

USA | Canada | UK | Ireland | Australia | New Zealand | India | South Africa | China

penguin.com
A Penguin Random House Company

Original Title: Agatha Mistery: Missione Safari
Text by Sir Steve Stevenson
Original cover and illustrations by Stefano Turconi

English language edition copyright © 2015 Penguin Group (USA) LLC. Original edition published by Istituto Geografico De Agostini S.p.A., Italy, 2012 © 2012 Atlantyca Dreamfarm s.r.l., Italy

International Rights © Atlantyca S.p.A.—via Leopardi 8, 20123 Milano, Italia
foreignrights@atlantyca.it—www.atlantyca.com

Published in 2015 by Grosset & Dunlap, a division of Penguin Young Readers Group, 345 Hudson Street, New York, New York 10014. GROSSET & DUNLAP is a trademark of Penguin Group (USA) LLC. Printed in the USA.

Library of Congress Cataloging-in-Publication Data is available.

ISBN 978-0-448-48679-6

10 9 8 7 6 5 4 3 2 1

Agatha

Girl of Mystery

The Kenyan Expedition

by Sir Steve Stevenson
illustrated by Stefano Turconi

translated by Siobhan Tracey
adapted by Maya Gold

Grosset & Dunlap
An Imprint of Penguin Group (USA) LLC

EIGHTH MISSION
Agents

Agatha
Twelve years old, an
aspiring mystery writer;
has a formidable memory

Dash
Agatha's cousin and student
at the private school Eye
International Detective Academy

Chandler
Butler and former boxer with impeccable British style

Watson
Obnoxious Siberian cat with the nose of a bloodhound

Haida
Short-haired and athletic, manages the Outer Limits Safari Agency

DESTINATION

Kenya

OBJECTIVE

Retrieve a rare white giraffe,
mysteriously vanished from
the Masai Mara National
Reserve, in the wild savanna

The Investigation Begins . . .

In a central-London penthouse packed full of high-tech devices lived Dashiell Mistery, an aspiring detective with a passion for technology. He was not an organized person, and pieces of his collection often met with unfortunate ends: an MP3 player frozen in the freezer, a laptop drowned in the bathtub, a video-game controller liquefied in the microwave . . .

Only one object was worthy of Dash's full attention: his EyeNet, a valuable tool that the Eye International Detective Academy—Dash's school—provided for its students. The EyeNet was a mass of futuristic features encased in a

titanium shell, and the young Londoner kept it hanging above the sofa so that it was never out of his sight.

One Saturday afternoon in late April, Dash was busy tinkering with an old radio with bent antennae. The floor was already a chaotic mess of electronic components, wires, transistors, and other materials recovered from unused appliances. While carefully removing the internal circuits and putting them on the carpet, he continually flicked his gaze at the EyeNet to check that it was in its place. It was two o'clock. Dash put the old radio aside to hurriedly scoff down a sandwich before moving on to his next project.

The previous week, he had taken a videoconference course in Subterfuge and Escapes, a discipline detailing techniques for getting oneself off the hook using only talent and whatever tools were at hand. The instructor for

the course, code name GC43, was nicknamed MacGyver in honor of the famous television series.

Dash had subsequently thrown himself headlong into the study of electronics and a frenzy of new projects. With the radio dismantled, Dash's main task for today was to record the notes from his electric guitar directly onto his computer using wiring of his own invention. He completed the final steps and hoisted his gleaming red guitar by the neck, adopting a rock-star pose.

He inserted the plug into the computer. Squinting at his monitor to check the frequencies, he positioned his hands on the strings and launched into a Led Zeppelin solo.

SBRANGGGGGG!!!

The speakers let out a noise so loud that it made the glass in his fifteenth-floor windows vibrate. The shock wave threw the slender boy across the

room, and a stunned expression covered his face. "I for-forgot to unplug the st-stereo system!" he exclaimed to himself.

As if that weren't enough, a piercing alarm suddenly sounded, followed by a panicked shout. He had frightened the other inhabitants of Baker Palace nearly to death!

"I have to do something!" he cried, pushing a mess of electronics under the table. "If they figure out it was me, I'm done for!"

He covered the jumbled pile with a sheet, barely a moment before there was a knock at the door.

"Dash Mistery!" someone called. "It was you—that noise came from in there!"

"Get out here and face the music!" someone added.

Judging from the angry voices, it seemed that a line of protestors had filled the hallway.

Dash ran his hands through his disheveled hair and approached the door with cautious steps. "Who is it?" he asked innocently.

A chorus of complaints sounded from outside. Dash released the security chain and peered out just enough to see at least twenty people crowded near his door. He gulped. "Did you feel that terrible earthquake, too?" he asked. "It's all over the news . . ."

"Don't mess around with us!" shouted the landlord of the building, a gray-haired lawyer

wearing a suit of the same color. "You're in enough trouble as it is!" He waved a piece of paper under Dash's nose. It could only be an eviction notice. "This is the last straw, Mr. Mistery," he added sternly.

Dash's legs turned to jelly. "But, I-I—" he stammered. "I didn't do anything!"

"The electric guitar!" interrupted the neighbor from the apartment directly below, a woman with a shrill voice who worked in finance. "I heard that demonic instrument just before the alarm went off!"

"I wasn't playing a guitar. I don't even own one, trust me!"

More complaints erupted. "He's telling lies! The regulations prohibit musical instruments! Evict him!" shouted a chorus of the elegant building's tenants.

"We need proof," the landlord interrupted, trying to calm tempers. "Let me in, Mr. Mistery. I

would like to see for myself that you don't have a guitar."

"Um . . . of course . . . come in."

The man entered and inspected the room with hawk-like eyes. "Where is it hidden?" he growled. "Under the sheet?"

The young detective shrugged. "Take a look, if you like. It's just a bunch of circuits and other equipment. I work with advanced electronics," he said with indifference, reclining on the sofa. The soft cushions hid the shape of the guitar.

The search continued for several long minutes, but in the end the landlord had to give up. "Very well, Mr. Mistery," he declared in disappointment. "Without the offending item, I can't evict you."

"What did I tell you?" Dash grinned, gesturing toward the door from his spot on the couch. Just then, the EyeNet began flashing furiously. It was his school, signaling that he had a new mission!

Dash grabbed the EyeNet, threw on a jacket, and slipped out past the other tenants, who were still grumbling on the crowded landing. He pulled the door closed tightly behind him and ran for the elevator.

As he reached the elevator, he checked the EyeNet screen. "An investigation in Kenya?" he shrieked.

Fortunately for him, he knew exactly where to find his cousin and incomparable companion in adventure, Agatha Mistery.

CHAPTER ONE
At Portobello Market

A fresh breeze swept away the thick London smog. Agatha Mistery took a deep breath, feeling bubbly and energized. She was striding across Portobello Road, home of the world-famous flea market in Notting Hill, on her way to meet her favorite antiques dealer.

Beside her stood Chandler, the Mistery family's jack-of-all-trades butler. Chandler had once been a professional heavyweight boxer, and his imposing size helped to part the crowd of Londoners and tourists. The road was packed with colorful stalls and shops selling all kinds of wares: vintage clothes and spectacular hats,

paintings of every style and era, gold and silver jewelry, old coffeepots, antique cameras with bellows, and all sorts of knickknacks. On every side of them, customers shouted at the top of their lungs as they admired the goods on display and tried to snatch up the best deals.

"We really should come here more often," said Agatha, swiveling her head to drink everything in. "Portobello Market has such a magical atmosphere!"

"Do you really think so, Miss?" replied the butler, loosening his collar. "Don't you find it a bit crowded and airless?"

"It's the biggest antiques market in the world," said Agatha. "That's why it's so popular. Everyone's hoping to find hidden treasures!"

Chandler couldn't wait to return to the peace and quiet of Mistery House. He picked up his pace. "I think I've spotted the stall you're looking for, just up ahead," he said. "The Shelves

of Monsieur Truffaut, isn't that it?"

Agatha took his arm. "Good eye, Chandler," she said with a grin. They'd been there many times before, but she knew the butler wanted to wind up their errand as quickly as possible. "Come on. Off we go."

It was already past four o'clock and the stalls would be closing soon. Agatha needed a new notebook, and Monsieur Truffaut specialized in early-twentieth-century bound books, produced by French craftsmen for Parisian stationery stores. The same style of notebooks had been used by great writers such as Oscar Wilde and Ernest Hemingway, and Agatha wanted to become a great writer herself. To be more precise, she wanted to become a great *mystery* writer. That's why the shelves of her bedroom were stuffed with notebooks she'd filled up with curious details, plot outlines, and character descriptions.

She chose a notebook and showed it to

Chandler, listing all its features. "Soft leather cover, ivory deckled pages, hand-sewn binding, rounded corners, ribbon bookmark, and an elastic band to keep it closed," she said, beaming. "It's perfect!"

The butler nodded. "The best in the shop, Miss."

Agatha thanked the taciturn Monsieur Truffaut and left the store, inhaling the fragrance of paper with total delight. "I'm going to start working on a new story right away," she said. "As long as I don't get distracted by—"

Before she could finish her sentence, she ran into two females, almost identical except for a slight difference in height. They both had platinum blond hair and wore designer jackets, short skirts, and high-heeled boots. It was her school friend, Jessica, and Jessica's mother.

"Agatha, darling, what a surprise!" chirped Jessica, giving her an exaggerated hug. "You're

shopping at Portobello, too! What have you bought? Any finds?"

Overcome by the cloud of perfume around mother and daughter, Chandler turned away politely to cover a cough.

Before Agatha could respond, Jessica pulled out the hats she'd just bought, gushing over each one as Agatha did her best to sound enthusiastic.

Fashion was not one of the young writer's interests.

Glancing at her diamond watch, Jessica's mother interrupted impatiently. "Hurry up, Jessica! You've got to get ready for the gala tonight and we'll need at least three hours for makeup and hair!"

Agatha jumped at the chance to end the conversation. "I'd hate to make you late," she told Jessica with a wry smile. "See you at school!"

"Oh, school!" grumbled Jessica's mother. "My daughter apparently thinks it's an haute couture fashion show."

Annoyed, Jessica picked up her bags and got ready to leave. But first she asked, "Agatha, sweetie, what's that cute cousin of yours called again? Rush? Flash?"

"Dash," Agatha corrected her. "Why do you ask?"

"I saw him about half an hour ago at the

market entrance. He said he was looking for you!"

"Really?" Agatha snapped to attention.

Jessica let out a giggle. "He was 'dashing' around like a maniac," she said. "He's got such adorable hair . . ."

Agatha did not answer. In a flash, she and Chandler had disappeared from the mother's and daughter's view, burrowing into the crowd.

"He must have a new mission!" Agatha exclaimed. "Thank goodness I told Dash last night we were going to Portobello!"

Chandler planted his feet, taking advantage of his height to survey the crowd. "How will we find him in all this confusion, Miss?" he asked.

Agatha bit her lip and began thinking out loud. "Well, if he arrived half an hour ago, he's probably been up and down the whole market at least once," she reflected. "Knowing how lazy Dash is, it wouldn't surprise me if he was already taking a break . . ."

"But where? I don't see any benches!"

"You're forgetting his sweet tooth," said Agatha with a laugh. She looked around, then pointed at a sign. "I bet he's sipping hot chocolate in that café over there!"

They both took off through the obstacle course of stalls. The market was closing at five, but the crowds hadn't thinned. As soon as they reached the café, they peered in through the window.

Inside, Dash was hunched over a steaming cup of cocoa in a corner of the room. Looking lost and forlorn, he bit into a doughnut and checked his EyeNet with a sigh.

Glad her assumption had proven correct, Agatha rushed to his table. "Never fear, cousin dear! We've got your back!" she said, greeting him with a smile.

Dash swallowed quickly, nearly choking with surprise. Chandler had to give him a couple of quick karate chops between his shoulder blades.

As soon as he could breathe again, Dash jumped to his feet like a spring.

"A mission in Kenya, can you believe it?" he cried. "The plane leaves at six. We don't have a moment to lose!"

He was shouting so loudly that everyone in the café turned to stare. "You've got to stop playing those spy video games," Agatha said, covering up Dash's outburst. She and Chandler ushered him to the door with embarrassed grins.

Once they were safely outside, she lowered her voice. "How do you think we could get to the airport in less than an hour? We have to go back to Mistery House, pack our suitcases, put Watson in his cat carrier, and study the files on the mission!"

"Master Dash, did you check to see if there's a later flight?" Chandler asked.

The young detective was always panicked about school assignments, and the realization

that he was about to miss his plane was the nail in the coffin. He stood paralyzed, staring at the colorful terrace houses on Portobello Road, ignoring the crowds milling past.

Agatha sighed and passed a hand in front of his eyes. "Earth to Dash, anyone home?" she joked. "Check your EyeNet for flights leaving later tonight. There's no point getting upset if there is another."

Dash whipped out the EyeNet and began clicking away. "Nope," he moaned after a few moments of searching. "It's no use . . ."

"Let me see," said his cousin.

Agatha immediately saw that there were no more flights to Nairobi, Kenya's capital, until the next morning. She tried calming Dash down. "We'll sleep at my house and catch the five a.m. tomorrow, nice and refreshed!" she said cheerfully.

Chandler raised a skeptical eyebrow. "Five in the morning?"

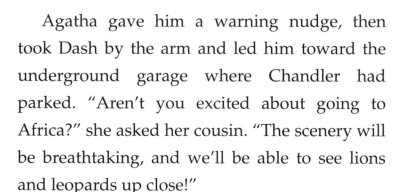

Agatha gave him a warning nudge, then took Dash by the arm and led him toward the underground garage where Chandler had parked. "Aren't you excited about going to Africa?" she asked her cousin. "The scenery will be breathtaking, and we'll be able to see lions and leopards up close!"

Unfortunately, she'd overlooked the fact that Dash was terrified of cats, and she had to endure his vast repertoire of moans, groans, mumbles, and grumbles all the way home.

The White Giraffe

*O*t was just before dinner, and Agatha stared out the window at the storm that had suddenly rolled in. The patter of rain on the lavender roof of the Victorian manor mingled with the crackling fire in the fireplace, creating a cozy and peaceful atmosphere.

"According to the nature magazines I read, the rainy season just started," she murmured.

Standing beside her, Dash said, "Aren't you being a little dramatic? It's only a drizzle . . ."

Agatha laughed. "Actually, I was talking about Kenya," she said. "We'll need appropriate clothes for wildly different temperatures during

the days and nights, along with waterproof boots and some other precautions."

"Now you're opening those famous memory drawers!" Dash teased.

Just then, Chandler announced that the barbecued spareribs were ready, and both kids sat down at the table. Watson, Agatha's white Siberian cat, strolled into the room, lured by the enticing smell of smoked meat. He rubbed against Agatha's legs until Chandler served him his own mini-ribs on a silver platter.

The butler removed his checkered apron and sat at the head of the table, wishing everyone "Bon appétit!"

The White Giraffe

Agatha's parents were always going away on globe-trotting business trips and entrusted Chandler with running the Victorian mansion on the outskirts of London. This meant that he was the one who accompanied his young mistress on her exciting adventures.

"I downloaded the mission file," said Dash, gnawing a rib. "But before we discuss the details, I'd like to watch the video clips on your dad's flat-screen."

Agatha sensed a hint of anxiety in his voice. She took a bite of her baked potato, then asked, "Is there something bothering you?"

"Yeah, there is," Dash said, nodding. He put down his bone. "Delaying our departure might have been a good thing, because this is a really challenging case."

Curious, Agatha nodded, inviting Dash to continue.

"The reason we've been contacted is pretty

bizarre," he said, sounding mysterious.

"What is it, Master Dash?" Chandler asked politely.

Dash wiped his chin with a napkin. "A white giraffe has gone missing, and we have to track it down in the middle of thousands of acres of wild savanna!" he explained with a half grin. "Don't you think that's a crazy request?"

Agatha tapped the tip of her nose with one finger. "A white giraffe?" she said, thinking aloud. "I remember reading that they're very rare. They're not true albinos, but an unusual coloring known as leucistic. Because they're so rare, many African tribes revere them as sacred . . ."

"You are too much," declared Dash, slightly envious. "You never miss a thing!"

His attention was grabbed by the giant platter of caramel flan that Chandler had brought to the table. After Dash greedily devoured his dessert, they headed to Arthur Mistery's study.

The White Giraffe

Even though Agatha's father never spent much time at home, his study, like all the other rooms in Mistery House, was in perfect order: spotless and recently dusted. The walls were covered with photos and memorabilia from all over the world, and the shelves groaned under piles of official documents in many languages.

Dash turned on the computer to play his first video clip on the oversize monitor. After the Eye International logo, a man with a bushy mustache and a bowler hat on his bald head appeared. It was the professor of Investigation Techniques, better known as UM60.

"This mission is perfect for you, Agent DM14," said the little man energetically. "Go immediately to the Masai Mara National Reserve, south of Nairobi, near the Tanzanian border. We've been contacted by two anthropologists, Patrick Lemonde and Annette Vaudeville, who have spent years following a Masai tribe to study their

traditional customs. As you'll see in the attached document, peace in the tribe has been marred by a terrible event. Resolve the situation at once, and enjoy a relaxing vacation, DM14."

The screen suddenly went black. The communication seemed to be over when the professor abruptly popped back onscreen. "Just kidding, Agent," he thundered. "No vacation! You have exactly one week to find out what happened, or fail!"

Agatha had already jumped up from her chair, deep in thought. She quickly returned to the leather sofa and started to organize their plan of action.

"What do we know about these anthropologists?" she asked.

Stretched out on the rug, Dash flipped through the case file and rattled off all the information he had. They were originally from Belgium, and a photo showed them in safari clothes, patting

an African rhinoceros. Patrick Lemonde was forty-five years old, with a sun-weathered face and squint lines. Annette Vaudeville, three years younger, was a vigorous-looking woman with hard features.

The scientific community considered them to be among the top anthropologists in their field of cultural studies. Apparently, they had managed

to contact and establish relations with a reclusive Masai tribe that still maintained a completely traditional lifestyle.

"This won't be an easy one," Agatha said.

Chandler frowned. "What do you mean, Miss?"

Dash looked even more anxious.

Agatha began to pace back and forth, holding one finger up in the air. "Well, the Masai are a proud warrior culture that was never subdued by colonial empires. You may have seen documentaries about their colorful red clothing, intricate beaded collars, and tribal dances. Traditionally, they were nomadic herdsmen, but in modern times many of them have established permanent villages." She paused for a moment to bring up some images from the case files on the computer screen, then went on with her lecture. "The reason this case is particularly delicate is the white giraffe. The Masai believe

in Enkai, a deity of a thousand colors, but the anthropologists claim the particular tribe they're studying worships this white giraffe, which was born near their village, on the advice of their village elder and *oloibon*, or spiritual guide."

Noting her companions' bewildered expressions, Agatha tried to explain better. "The giraffe's disappearance could seriously upset the balance in this Masai village," she summarized. "A tribe would feel lost without its deity, whatever form it may take."

Dash and Chandler exchanged looks, reassured now that they had a grasp of the basics.

"So how should we proceed?" asked Dash.

Agatha already had a clear plan. "First step? We all get some sleep!" She smiled. "But before we go to bed, we each have a job to do."

"What's that, Miss Agatha?" Chandler asked eagerly.

Within minutes, Agatha had decided that

Dash would read more about Masai traditions, Chandler would get busy packing their clothes and booking their five a.m. flight, and Agatha would contact a relative who could help them with their mission. They all took off in different directions, leaving Watson on the arm of the sofa, wondering what in the world was so urgent.

Left alone, the cat followed his mistress immediately. He found Agatha consulting an enormous globe covered with the contact details of all the Misterys around the world. "Oh dear," she said, running a finger over the names. "We have so many relatives in Kenya . . . Who will be the most suitable?"

It did not take her long to decide, and she was soon lifting the phone to call Haida Mistery, a fourth cousin who was a licensed safari guide. A guide of very special safaris, in fact.

Like all of the Misterys scattered all over the world, Haida had an unusual job. Her small

company in Nairobi was called the Outer Limits Safari Agency and offered extreme adventure trips: scaling the peak of Kilimanjaro, or exploring the marshy shores of Lake Victoria and the dense equatorial jungles. They offered a far more hands-on experience than the usual tourist safaris.

Even though Kenya was three time zones ahead of England, Haida answered the phone in her office and enthusiastically agreed to help them.

Her job accomplished, Agatha pulled Watson onto her lap and curled up to sleep under the soft blanket in her room. They'd be traveling toward the equator as soon as the sun rose!

A Pit Stop in Nairobi

Chandler had booked them a flight with KLM, a Dutch airline that made a stopover in Amsterdam. During the two-hour wait in Schiphol Airport before they continued their trip, Dash finally started to show the first signs of life.

"Wh-where are we?" he asked, blinking sleep-heavy eyelids. "Is this Africa?" His feet dragged as he stumbled along, holding on to the butler's mighty arm. It certainly wasn't the first time his companions had seen him stumble around like a sleep-deprived zombie, but this time his tiredness was well earned.

He'd stayed up all night poring over the case file documents, and then read an in-depth book about Kenya from Agatha's library.

Agatha, who was jotting down notes in the new notebook she'd bought on Portobello Road, guided him into a chair in the waiting room. "Go back to sleep. It won't be long now."

Chandler struggled to hold back a chuckle at Agatha's lie. In truth, they were less than halfway through their voyage, which would be eleven hours in total.

Their flight resumed without a hitch. Soon they were soaring over the blue Mediterranean Sea, then following the river Nile south, past the Valley of the Kings in Egypt, the site of their first adventure together. Agatha passed the time playing with Watson, watching the magnificent landscapes from the window, and reviewing her notes with Chandler. Eventually, she dozed off on her cousin's shoulder.

As they were landing at Jomo Kenyatta International Airport in Nairobi, Dash woke with a scream. "Ahhh! A hyena! It's on top of me!"

Agatha straightened her back and rubbed her eyes. "Someday I'd really like to find out what goes on in your head when you're sleeping," she said, feigning offense. She winked at Chandler. "Do I look like a hyena to you?"

"No, of course not, Miss," the butler replied promptly.

The three companions had prepared for the cool Kenyan nights, and pulled fleece jackets on over their sweaters and cargo shorts.

The humidity enveloped them as soon as they stepped off the plane. It was already well into the evening, and the giant red sun was dipping below the horizon.

As they retrieved their luggage, they were besieged by children offering to take them on safari. Dash, still sleep-dazed from the trip, kept waving "no" with his hand. Suddenly they were approached by a woman in her early thirties. She had short hair, an athletic build, and wore a camouflage-print uniform. She stared at him with intense dark eyes.

"What do you want?" asked the young detective. "We're in a bit of a hurry . . ."

"And where are you in such a hurry to go without me, Dashiell Mistery?" she demanded.

Dash was thrown off guard.

"You're . . . are you Haida?" he asked, stunned. He had never seen a photo of his muscular, beautiful African cousin.

Looking at Agatha, she announced solemnly, "Haida Mistery, at your service, Agent DM14!" Then she burst out laughing and hugged the new arrivals enthusiastically. "Hey, cousin!"

"I thought you were a soldier," explained Dash, wiping sweat from his forehead. "I guess your camouflage gear prevents animals from noticing you in the jungle . . ."

"The savanna!" Haida corrected him. "Grasslands, not vines. Agatha told me that we're heading south to the Masai Mara Reserve."

"Our dear Dash stayed up all night reading a huge illustrated guidebook about Kenya," Agatha chimed in with a friendly smile. "But clearly it hasn't done him much good!" Then she got more serious. "How about we get some dinner, find someplace to sleep tonight, and leave for Masai Mara first thing in the morning?"

Haida nodded, escorting the group toward the exit. "We can sleep at my office, though we'll have to rough it a bit. It's not very big, but I don't spend much time in the city. I prefer to sleep under the stars!"

They soon found out that she was telling the truth. After a meal of delicious chicken stew, rice, and yams, they went to the Outer Limits Safari Agency office. The agency was on a side street in central Nairobi and looked like a converted garage, with a small glass-walled room full of brochures, itineraries, and framed nature photos of exotic landscapes and animals.

"My customers are usually extreme-sports fanatics and thrill-seekers, but I'll take all possible safety precautions with you," said Haida, pointing at an ancient four-by-four truck. The Land Rover was splattered with mud, its interior covered with dust and dry twigs. Haida invited Chandler to add their luggage to the pile of camping equipment, canned food, and tanks of water and gas that she'd loaded before their arrival. Dash took a closer look at the vehicle. It had a sunroof and six seats, all torn and covered with sand. Judging from its shabby appearance, it looked like it had already crossed half of Africa!

They slept inside a small pop-up tent that Haida had set up in the back of the garage. A few minutes after wriggling into his sleeping bag, Dash asked shyly, "Could we open the screens a little? It's superhot in here!"

"At your own risk," said Haida, grinning.

Agatha pulled some insect repellent out of

her bag, spritzed her skin, and silently passed it to Chandler and Haida, while Dash stuck his head outside the tent flap.

"I recommend getting a bit of fresh air, guys!" exclaimed Dash. "It's nice and cool out here!"

At that moment, a swarm of mosquitoes and gnats took aim and started to bite him all over.

"It's an invasion!" he yelled, waving his arms like an octopus. "Zip up the tent or they'll eat us alive!"

Chandler zipped up the tent as everyone else had a laugh. Even Watson seemed amused.

"Consider that a lesson in the first rule of survival, Agent DM14," said Haida when the laughter died down. "Never underestimate the hidden dangers of African wildlife!"

Agatha took this as a chance to gather more information about the risks they might face on their mission. Haida was not a hunting guide, but she'd had close encounters with lions, leopards, elephants, black rhinos, and Cape buffalo during her extreme-sport adventures.

"The famous Big Five," Agatha commented, captivated by Haida's hair-raising stories. "The most dangerous animals on the African continent!"

"That's right," said Haida. "But don't

underestimate herd animals like wildebeest, zebras, and antelopes, and not just because you could end up under their hooves . . ."

". . . but also because they attract predators," Agatha finished her sentence.

Haida nodded agreement. "There are also vultures, snakes, crocodiles, hippos, and all kinds of venomous insects," she continued cheerfully, rolling onto her side. "To be honest, it's best if you don't leave the Land Rover without me tomorrow. I have a rifle for emergencies."

Dash gave a sigh. "Well, that's not going to help with those killer mosquitoes," he said. "But I swear I'll stick close by at all times and follow your advice to the letter!"

With this promise, the conversation ended and they all fell into a deep sleep.

They rose at dawn, splashed their faces with water, and hit the streets of Nairobi in the Land Rover. The city was a mixture of modern high-

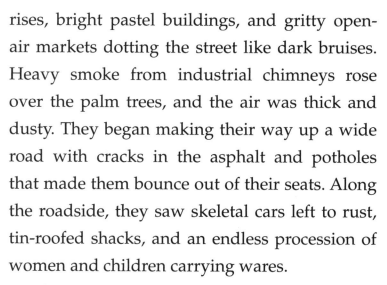

rises, bright pastel buildings, and gritty open-air markets dotting the street like dark bruises. Heavy smoke from industrial chimneys rose over the palm trees, and the air was thick and dusty. They began making their way up a wide road with cracks in the asphalt and potholes that made them bounce out of their seats. Along the roadside, they saw skeletal cars left to rust, tin-roofed shacks, and an endless procession of women and children carrying wares.

This bleak urban panorama pulled at the heartstrings of the wealthy Londoners, who looked out in silence until the landscape became wilder and full of color.

"This is where the parks and reserves begin," Haida warned. "It will take us another four or five hours to get to Masai Mara, barring any setbacks."

This was not an encouraging statement. Half an hour later, Watson began to meow in his

cat carrier, sniffing the air and looking around. Chandler smelled something strange as well and asked, "Do you smell something burning?"

The Land Rover screeched to a sudden halt. Haida threw open the door and jumped out, quickly followed by the others. Noxious fumes rose from the engine.

"Don't worry, it's just the oil," Haida reassured them. "Second rule of survival: Never travel without backup supplies."

While Haida changed the oil, Dash and Agatha took off their jackets. The temperature was rising with every minute and the sun baked down on their heads. Dash wanted to check the forecast on his EyeNet, and also make sure there was satellite reception this far from Nairobi. He took it out, fiddling with the keypad as Agatha stretched her legs. "Is it working all right?" she asked Dash.

"Perfect reception," he said with a grin. Then

he leaned in and whispered, "But I could sure do without this unplanned pit stop . . ."

"Don't worry, we're in good hands with Haida," Agatha said with a smile. "I trust any woman who knows how to change her own oil."

Dash looked out at the unbroken horizon, already shimmering with the heat. "Did you tell her about our secret mission?"

"Not the details," replied his cousin. "If you like, we can make up a cover story."

The student detective thought for a moment. "No, let's tell her everything. We'll need her expertise!" he decided. So for the rest of the journey they talked about the Masai, the Belgian anthropologists, and the strange case of the missing white giraffe.

Masai Mara

By noon, the Masai Mara National Reserve appeared in all its splendor. Haida stopped the Land Rover on an outcrop to allow the children to take in the majestic landscape.

The world seemed to be split in two; the turquoise sky arching above, and a vast valley of grass and umbrella-shaped acacia trees below.

Herds of wildebeest and zebras grazed in silence, ready to move at the slightest hint of danger. Flamingos crossed the sky.

Agatha took out her binoculars. "It feels like we've stepped a million years back in time," she whispered, her voice full of emotion.

While she and Dash gawked at the wildlife, Haida showed Chandler a few of her tricks for maintaining the Land Rover. He listened intently, petting Watson's fur. Watson was twitching, scratching, and yowling as he struggled to free himself. He was probably feeling the call of the wild and yearning to stalk some unseen African rodent. By the time they reassembled, everyone was smiling serenely and could not wait to get on with their mission. But first, they sat in the shade of the Land Rover, eating some canned meat and beans before they continued their trip.

At around three o'clock, the Masai village finally appeared from behind rolling hills. It was several miles off the dirt road, and Haida had to steer right through the tall grasses, bouncing along in low gear. "It's a risky maneuver," she confessed. "I don't recommend you try it at home!"

"Third rule of survival?" Dash asked dryly. His

joke made them laugh so hard that all the birds perched in a nearby acacia took flight. Pleased with himself, the young detective relaxed back into his seat and stretched his legs. "We make an incredible team, guys!" he gloated. "I bet the Masai will be delighted to see us, and we'll finish our investigation in no time!"

A few minutes later, Dash found out he was wrong. Very wrong.

Up ahead, ten Masai warriors emerged from the trees and commanded them to stop. They were wrapped in red tunics and all held sharp spears. Haida told her companions to stay put and went to speak with them in Swahili.

Dash and Agatha held their breath, while Chandler instinctively put his hand on the rifle in case anyone threatened Haida.

"*Oloibon!*" the warriors erupted in chorus at the end of the discussion, then one of them left the group and started toward the village at the

pace of a marathon runner.

Haida climbed back into the driver's seat, looking worried. "They won't let us go any farther," she said. "I tried to convince them we weren't tourists, but we have to wait in the Land Rover until the anthropologists arrive."

Before Dash could protest, Agatha spoke. "That's understandable. The tribe wants to maintain their own roots, and they don't take kindly to strangers poking around."

"So we're stuck here?" asked Dash. "Is there a rest stop somewhere in the area?"

"We're in the middle of the savanna," replied Haida, handing him a grease-stained map. "We'd have to drive several hours to the nearest tourist facility."

Agatha crossed her arms. "Fourth rule, dear cousin: Always bring patience!"

Time seemed to stand still, and an oppressive heat fell over them; insects buzzed and birds

called, but everything else was still.

Half an hour passed before the line of Masai warriors parted to allow three people to pass. The children saw a European man and a woman with sunburned skin, dressed in tribal clothing and jewelry.

It was Patrick Lemonde and Annette Vaudeville, along with an old man hunched over a stick and speaking in an incomprehensible dialect. The two anthropologists treated him with great respect, listening to his advice and dipping their heads with reverence. Only after the old man gave his consent did the pair of scholars approach the Land Rover.

"We were afraid you weren't coming," Patrick said. His face looked gaunter than his photograph in the case file.

Annette's sharp features pulled into a frown. "But you're just kids! Do you have any idea how much effort it took to convince the *oloibon*

we should bring in Eye International?" she said angrily.

Agatha took her reaction in stride. "Allow me to introduce the highly qualified Agent DM14," she said, pointing at Dash. "He is the one entrusted with conducting the investigation."

The two anthropologists exchanged dubious glances. "And the others? Are you his support team?" Lemonde wanted to know.

Haida quickly introduced the rest of the group, then gestured to Agatha, who immediately started to ask questions. "Where was the white giraffe last seen?" she asked, handing the anthropologists their map.

The anthropologists used a pen to circle the area where the giraffe herd was most often spotted. It encompassed a stand of acacias, a ridge of hills to the north, and the river that flowed along the outskirts of the village. "Hwanka would visit his tribe every morning to drink at

the river," Annette explained. "Afterward, the herd would go to a shaded area about here . . ." She circled an area a few miles from their current position.

"Hwanka?" Dash sounded surprised. "Is that the giraffe's name?"

"It means 'spirit of fortune,'" explained Patrick. "The *oloibon* believe that Hwanka's disappearance will bring the tribe great misfortune. But they also don't want humans to interfere with his fate . . ."

"Which means they haven't searched the area to find out what happened, am I right?" Agatha asked shrewdly.

The two anthropologists nodded. "We obey the villagers' rules," Annette continued. "As I told you, it was an uphill battle to convince the village elder to make a special allowance for you to come. But now that you're here . . ."

"What are we waiting for?" asked Dash,

excited. "Let's start looking for clues right away!"

At his prompting, Haida and Chandler quickly climbed into the Land Rover.

"Are you going to join the search?" Agatha asked the scholars before getting into the vehicle.

Annette hesitated, then stared at her colleague, taking his hand. "Go with them," she whispered. "The *oloibon* has agreed to accept their help. If you bring back Hwanka, they'll welcome you as a hero!"

They embraced quickly, and Patrick joined Agatha on the back seat. The four-by-four backed up and moved off across the grasslands, under the silent gaze of the Masai warriors and their elder wise man.

"Are we certain that Hwanka wasn't attacked by lions, leopards, or hyenas?" Chandler asked.

"Highly unlikely," Haida replied. "Predators don't attack giraffes."

Everyone waited for Patrick Lemonde to

confirm this, but it was Agatha who stepped in. "It's no doubt the work of poachers," she declared, studying the map resting on her knees. "They wanted to capture the white giraffe and laid a trap somewhere deep in the scrub, where the herd likes to rest and the Masai warriors won't go for fear of disturbing them."

She scratched the tip of her nose and indicated a precise area to Haida. "I bet we'll find a camp, tire tracks, and other signs of an ambush."

"What makes you so sure?" asked Dash.

"News of a rare white giraffe would no doubt attract the attention of poachers, dear cousin," she explained. "And Professor Lemonde will confirm that other giraffes have been taken within the park's boundaries in recent weeks . . ."

Patrick looked stunned by Agatha's thorough research. "I'm no expert on poaching, but the young lady may have a plausible theory," he agreed. "I'd like to add that while rifle shots can

be heard for miles, tranquilizer darts are silent. I'd assume these poachers knocked Hwanka out so they could take him alive."

Haida bit her lip in a rage. "Giraffes are a protected species," she hissed. "We have to catch whoever did this at all costs!"

She stepped on the accelerator and shifted into a higher gear, racing a bumpy path across the vast plains as antelopes, zebras, and wildebeest sprang out of their way.

They soon reached the area Agatha had suggested. Her theory about poachers proved to be correct.

"Look, I see tire tracks!" Dash exclaimed, pointing out the window.

Agatha nodded. "The mud still looks fresh, so they can't be more than a few days old."

"Those blackened stones must be from a fire," added Chandler.

Patrick Lemonde pointed at the acacia grove,

where several giraffes stood stretching their necks to eat leaves. "That looks like the rest of his herd!" he said happily.

Over the next few minutes, they searched far and wide for clues. Dash used his EyeNet to photograph close-ups of all the tire tracks and search for a vehicle match.

It was six o'clock in the evening and their hunt for the poachers had just begun!

A Series of
Unfortunate Clues

$\mathcal{A}$gatha called the others together to assess their findings. "All right, we've found cartridge cases from tranquilizer darts, footprints from four or five people, tire tracks from a jeep and a heavyweight truck, and some ropes and nets left on the ground," she reported. "But I think the most curious clue we have so far in this investigation is this container."

She passed Dash a small tin box she'd recovered near the ashes of the fire. He observed it from all angles and gave it a shake. "What's so special about it?" he asked, unable to draw any conclusions.

"Well, first of all, open it," she suggested.

Dash obeyed. "That's what I thought! It's empty!" he yelled. "Nothing inside but a strong smell of tea . . ."

"Excellent, Dash!" smiled the girl. "If I'm not mistaken, it's a fine blend of black Ceylon."

"And what does that tell you?" Patrick Lemonde interrupted.

"Did you notice the inscription engraved on the lid?" asked Agatha.

Haida carefully lifted the lid and read aloud, "'A Commendation from the Most Honorable Society of British Gentlemen.'"

Everybody was speechless.

"But how does this help, Miss?" asked Chandler, confused. "There are thousands of groups like that in England."

"But we're in Kenya, not England," replied Agatha. "It's time to consult Dash's prized gadget," she announced with a smile. "Let's

cross-reference all the information we have, and see if the Eye International archives can make a connection."

"Great idea!" said Dash, pulling out his EyeNet. Then he paused, scratching his cheek. "How should I do this exactly? What should I search for?"

Haida Mistery, who was learning about investigative methodology very quickly, kindly moved to his side. "Type in the inscription and see what comes up."

"Of course!" he said. "We'll have the results in a moment . . ."

His face suddenly went pale. "Of all the times to lose the satellite signal!" he exclaimed. "I'll have to go to higher ground! Wait here!" He started to sprint through the knee-deep grass toward a raised outcropping a short distance away. It was a perfect hiding place for lions.

"Come back, Dash! It's dangerous!" yelled

Haida. Paralyzed with fear, the others joined in, yelling, "Stop, Dash! Turn back!"

Their cries were drowned out by the sudden thunder of hooves that spread over the valley. The ground shook as if there was an earthquake, and a herd of wildebeest stampeded across the savanna, separating Dash from the rest of the group.

A small but ferocious feline launched itself into the midst of the thundering dust cloud, and the herd of large animals veered off and thundered away. When the ground stopped moving, Dash told the others what had just happened. He was unharmed, but shaking like a leaf.

"If it weren't for Watson, I would have been crushed by those terrible hooves," he said in a wobbly voice. "He leaped right in front of me, and the wildebeest must have mistaken him for a lion cub."

"Where there's a cub, there's a lioness." Haida nodded.

"So when they saw Watson, they all changed direction!"

Everyone turned to look at the cat, who was licking his paw nonchalantly. His white fur had turned mustard from the flying dust.

"Watson, I didn't know you loved Dash so

much!" said Agatha happily, smothering her pet with hugs.

Chandler's square jaw shook with emotion. "I'll give our courageous knight a double serving of kibble this evening, Miss Agatha," he said gravely.

Haida wanted to grab Dash by the ears and scream at him, but he had already charged back up the hill and was frantically entering data into his EyeNet.

"Did you find anything?" Patrick Lemonde asked anxiously when he returned a few minutes later. They were all on tenterhooks.

Dash shook his head, disappointed. "It was an exclusive gentlemen's club that closed its doors in the sixties, when English colonization ended," he grumbled. "I have a long list of former members, with photos, but it's hundreds of people."

"We need to narrow our search," said Agatha. "Ideas, anyone?"

"Could we ask the park authorities for help?" ventured Chandler. "They have rangers patrolling this whole reserve looking for poachers. Perhaps they might recognize one of the faces in the photos."

Patrick Lemonde pointed out that the authorities could easily include an accomplice or somebody else who could throw them off track. Haida agreed, bitterly adding that corruption was rampant among the park rangers. They decided to return to the Land Rover and heat up some soup on the fire. The sun was already low in the sky and dark rain clouds were beginning to gather.

Agatha got up to have another look at the tire marks left by the poachers, which grew faint where the sun-dried mud yielded to stonier ground. She scanned the horizon. "Do you think they would have taken a particular route?" she asked Haida.

Haida studied her map. "Quite often the smaller routes aren't even marked," she murmured. "And they'd want to stay out of sight. But we could follow their tire tracks as far as we can and then reassess the situation."

This seemed like a good idea to the rest, and they set off just as the first raindrops started to fall.

With the rain came trouble. First, the tailgate of the Land Rover flew open when they hit a bump. Their supplies scattered into the mud and they all got drenched picking everything up. As if that weren't enough, a mile or so later they got a flat tire and had to stop to change it. Everything took much longer than expected because of the heavy rain. They worked with clenched jaws, slipping often as the dry ground turned to deep mud, obscuring the tracks they were trying to follow. To add insult to injury, the downpour stopped as soon as they finally got back in the

vehicle. They'd wasted two hours and the sky was darkening fast.

"The poachers have a few days' head start," Agatha said, thinking aloud. "But transporting a live giraffe over uncharted roads would be slow and tricky."

Haida made a quick mental calculation. "If we don't hit any more snags, we can probably travel at twice their speed," she declared. "The problem is knowing which direction they went,

now that the storm's washed away all the tire tracks."

"What is a 'lodge'?" Dash asked, staring at the rain-soaked map.

"It's a tourist hotel with tents and viewing platforms for travelers on safari adventures," replied Agatha. Then her eyes lit up like lanterns. "Dash, you're a genius!" she exclaimed.

"Me?" Dash sounded astonished.

"We can ask for information at the lodge," Agatha continued, speaking quickly. "Maybe the poachers stopped for supplies, or someone on the staff noticed their truck passing through. Is it far?"

"I can't really tell," Dash said, lost. "Haida?"

Haida squinted at the map. Then, without a word, she pushed the Land Rover as fast as the darkness and mud would allow.

When they finally reached the hard-packed dirt driveway, they all breathed a sigh of relief.

They drove straight to a lodge called Big Sea in honor of the boundless grass sea of the Masai Mara.

There were tourist bungalows and touring jeeps with pop-up roofs parked outside the main lodge. While Haida, Chandler, and Dash waited inside the Land Rover, Agatha ran to question the tourist center employees. As she suspected, the lodge's head chef had seen a jeep and tall truck passing through. They stopped for gas, food, and water, then set off into the savanna. "And no tip for the waiter," he said with a frown.

"Can you describe what they looked like?" Agatha asked innocently. "We've lost track of our friends and can't reach them by phone. We need to know if these are the same people," she lied, adding, "though our friends always leave a good tip."

The chef gave her a detailed description. The group's leader was a white-haired Englishman

with a handlebar mustache that drooped past his chin; he was wearing a hunting cap. He had three assistants, dressed in the khaki pants commonly worn on tobacco plantations.

It was enough.

Agatha rejoined her companions and asked Dash to show her the photos he'd downloaded onto his EyeNet. There was only one white-haired man with a handlebar mustache.

"We've got you, John McDuff!" she exclaimed excitedly.

"Who in the world is that?" muttered her cousin.

"Our mysterious poacher!" said Agatha, smiling.

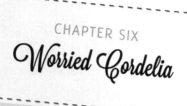

Worried Cordelia

*S*ince it was too dark to continue, they stopped for the night, pitching their tent near the lodge. They woke up early and sped westward, toward the tobacco plantations. Having consulted the Eye International archives, they'd discovered that McDuff had an extensive estate there.

They followed the highway that stretched from Nairobi to a large port city overlooking the Indian Ocean called Mombasa.

"We're nearly there," Haida advised them around noon, lifting her hands off the steering wheel to stretch her stiff arms.

"Thank goodness," said Dash, who was pale

as a sheet from the Land Rover's high-speed ride on the bumpy road. "I don't think I can take too much more of this."

"Focus on the information we've gathered about John McDuff," Agatha advised him. "There's still something that isn't quite right . . ."

The road cut through fields of chest-high plants with broad leaves that reflected the sun like green mirrors. There were open sheds where more of the giant leaves had been hung up to dry.

"That's a lot of tobacco," whispered Chandler, wiping the sweat from his forehead. "If there was a fire, we'd all be smoked."

John McDuff's boundless plantation was dotted with small groups of workers in khaki pants, broken-down trucks, and huts with thatched roofs.

The ground sloped gently upward to form a small hill. A large colonial villa with whitewashed walls stood at the top.

"We made it," Haida said with a grin. She stopped the Land Rover in front of the columned porch. A moment later, a large lady rushed out the front door. She was wearing a lacy cream dress, and a fancy hat covered her flyaway wisps of gray hair.

"JOHN! JOHN!" the woman shouted, her cheeks flushed bright pink. "You cannot spend so long away from home at your age! I was worried to death!"

She put on a pair of glasses, looked at the four-by-four in confusion, and only then noticed Agatha, Dash, and the others.

"You aren't my John," she mumbled, confused.

"I should say not," replied Agatha, jumping down from the Land Rover. "Actually, to be honest, we're trying to find him, too."

"Are you friends of John's, dear children?" she asked in a trembling voice.

"I should say not," Dash muttered, echoing

Agatha. Fortunately, the elderly woman didn't hear him.

As they'd learned from their research, the slightly dazed woman was named Cordelia, and she was John McDuff's wife. As soon as she spied Watson, she scooped him up in her arms and cuddled him to her chest, scratching him behind his ears and cooing endearments. The cat seemed to appreciate this, and started to purr.

"What an adorable kittums! You will be my guests, ladies and gentlemen! Any friend of my John is most welcome," Cordelia said happily, not even waiting for introductions. "I'll ask the cook to prepare you a delicious lunch!" She led them inside the grand villa.

Someone less observant than Agatha would have realized instantly that this was the home of an experienced hunter. There were animal skins and trophy heads everywhere, though some of the specimens looked a bit musty. Polished

hardwoods and pure white curtains were the dominant colors in every room. In the dining room, the group was invited to sit at a large teak table as the villa's staff carried in a selection of old-school British lunch dishes like steak and kidney pie, roast grouse, and smoked eel.

"Umm . . . your trophy collection is . . . really something," stammered Dash to break the silence. Chandler reached for a Cornish meat pasty.

Mrs. McDuff dabbed her eyes with the corner of a handkerchief. "Hunting was my dear John's greatest pleasure," she moaned, wiping away a tear.

It was the perfect opening to steer the conversation to the topic on all their minds.

"Why are you crying, Madam?" asked Patrick Lemonde. "Has something unpleasant happened to Mr. McDuff?"

"My John disappeared a week ago! And I can imagine why!" The group listened eagerly,

waiting for more. In response, she pulled a small bottle out of her pocket and rattled the pills inside it. "He has a heart condition, my poor husband," she cried in despair. "He shouldn't be tiring himself out in this beastly hot sun. But knowing him, he's gone off on some reckless hunting expedition, as he used to do with his old chums from the Most Honorable Society of British Gentlemen!"

Agatha shot a knowing look at her companions. Cordelia let out a long sigh, with Watson still clutched in her arms, and a cup of tea in her trembling hand. Agatha inhaled sharply. The scent was exactly the same as the Ceylon blend they had found in the tin box.

That makes perfect sense, but how do we proceed with the investigation? thought the girl. She hadn't expected Cordelia to have no idea where her husband was.

As Agatha tapped the tip of her nose, lost in

thought, Cordelia McDuff continued her story. She told them how she'd begged her husband to give up his hunting safaris and dedicate himself to the tobacco plantation. After much hesitation, John had agreed just to please her and hung up his hunting rifle for good. Everything had gone smoothly until a few weeks ago, when he received a strange letter. Ever since then, he had been agitated and impatient with her. Cordelia had come across him polishing his old double-barreled shotgun. Then later that night, he had disappeared with three trusted assistants, taking the jeep and a cargo truck from the plantation.

"I'm certain he's gone off on some wild expedition." She let out a deep sigh. "But he's not a young man anymore. His reflexes aren't what they once were, and his vision is poor. And on top of everything else, he forgot his heart medication. If he goes without it for too long, he might die!"

Worried Cordelia

A flash of cleverness lit up Agatha's eyes. "We can bring him his heart pills, Mrs. McDuff," she reassured her with a warm smile. "But we'd like to see the strange letter you mentioned. That might help us to find him faster."

Chandler and Dash raised their eyebrows in recognition of this brilliant strategy. Haida smiled, while Patrick Lemonde looked unsettled.

Cordelia put down her teacup and led them through the halls of the villa to a heavy door with a pair of spiraling antelope horns mounted above it.

"This is my husband's office. I don't know where he put the letter. I looked on his desk, but to no avail. In any case, if he kept it, it must be in here," she said.

Dash was the first across the threshold, where he found himself facing a lifelike stuffed lion crouched on the rug. It had massive paws, razor-sharp claws, and a mane the color of flames. As

soon as the boy set foot in McDuff's office, the beast jumped to its feet and opened its jaws in a fearsome *ROARRR!*

"ARRRRRGH!" yelled Dash, stumbling backward, smack into Chandler's large form.

"Don't worry, young man," Cordelia exclaimed with a chuckle. "That's Elwood, my husband's pet lion. We raised him from a cub. He's old and completely harmless . . . but he's a fantastic guard. Gave you a scare, eh?"

"Y-you . . . you could say that," stuttered Dash as the old woman petted the majestic king of the jungle on the nose. Even Watson looked impressed.

John McDuff's office was sun-filled and bright, with a wide baobab table and wicker club chairs. A magnificent collection of antique spears and other African weapons decorated the walls.

A leather writing pad, ink pot, and fountain pen lay on the desk, along with a paperweight made from a wildebeest hoof and an assortment of letters.

"Try checking his mail," said Cordelia, handing Chandler the pile of pages. "Perhaps I missed something. I get so muddled."

The Mistery House butler took the papers politely, then passed them to Dash.

While the young detective carefully studied each envelope, Agatha started searching the room.

"Nothing interesting here," mumbled Dash after he'd sorted through all the pages. "Business correspondence and bills. We're back to square one!"

"Don't worry," Agatha calmed him, holding up a small slip of paper. "The mysterious letter was hidden behind this carved shield!"

It wasn't a full letter, but a brief telegram which read:

TRANSPORT FOR WHITE GIRAFFE ORGANIZED STOP FERRY BRIGHT STAR LEAVES MOMBASA AT 19:15 TUESDAY APRIL 28 STOP PAYMENT ON RECEIPT STOP SIGNED PRINCE H.F.S.

"Prince H.F.S.?" asked Patrick Lemonde.

"Ferry *Bright Star*?" echoed Haida.

"White giraffe?" cried Cordelia McDuff, more worried than ever.

"It's perfectly clear," said Agatha. "This Prince

H.F.S. hired John McDuff to capture Hwanka the giraffe, and they'll ship him out from Mombasa tonight!"

"I was right, he went hunting!" groaned Cordelia. "I beg you, please, take the pills to my husband before he gets onto that ferry!"

"We will, but there's not much time," said Chandler, eyeing the clock. "No matter how fast Haida drives, we can't get to Mombasa by sundown."

Cordelia McDuff smiled enigmatically. "Come with me, my dears."

She escorted them outside the villa to an unused tobacco shed. Inside, they found a vintage biplane painted yellow, with a wooden propeller and two seats in the fuselage. The canvas wings were dusty and the wheels of the landing gear looked a bit flat, but all in all it looked ready for takeoff.

"Dash, Watson, and I can squeeze into the

passenger seats," Agatha evaluated. "Chandler can fly it, since he's the one with a pilot's license."

"Um, one of the ones," Haida said with a grin. "I fly skydiver clients around all the time."

"And what about me?" frowned Patrick Lemonde, looking anxious.

"No worries," Haida soothed him. "Chandler can fly it. My Land Rover may not be as fast as a plane, but if we get started right now, we can meet them in Mombasa by dawn!"

A Race Against Time

$\mathcal{H}$aida Mistery gave Chandler some final directions before she and Patrick Lemonde drove off at top speed, disappearing into the plantation's green fields.

It was two in the afternoon when they dragged the old yellow biplane out of the shed.

Cordelia McDuff watched the whole operation, continuously repeating how worried she was about her poor husband. Taking off, however, was no simple task.

"Want me to start the propeller?" Dash grinned as Chandler checked the controls. "Piece of cake!"

"Are you sure you can do it by yourself?" Agatha was doubtful.

"Sure thing!" Dash replied, reaching out to grab the large wooden propeller on the nose of the plane. "Watch my moves!"

The young detective signaled Chandler to get ready, then took a deep breath and pushed down on a propeller blade with all his strength. He hadn't realized it would be so heavy, nor did he know it was spring-loaded. The kickback sent him head over heels in the air. Cordelia squealed and the assembled workers burst out laughing.

It took Chandler's steely muscles to spin the propeller. Finally the engine sputtered to life and the biplane rolled across the estate's wide lawn, ready for takeoff.

The biplane banked at low altitude, circling back over Mrs. McDuff, who waved her handkerchief at them. "Don't forget to give John his medicine!" they heard her shriek.

Chandler straightened the joystick and the plane flew due east, toward the beaches of Mombasa.

Squeezed into the passenger seat, Agatha and Dash watched as the landscape became smaller and smaller. Even Watson leaned over to gaze at the great herds of migrating animals crossing the savanna.

Seen from above, Kenya was an endless succession of colors: grass-green valleys and red earth, plateaus ascending to peaks, silvery lakes, and patches of lush vegetation stretching for miles. The shadowy peaks of the mountains stretched up into cotton-wool clouds, and a waterfall cascaded down to a rushing stream below.

The view was magnificent.

Agatha and Dash couldn't contain their excitement. Even Chandler, who was usually perfectly stone-faced, found his eyes bulging

with awe behind his aviation goggles.

"Dash, we should get back to work," Agatha said after half an hour. She had to shout into her cousin's ear to be heard above the noisy engine.

"What work?" asked the young detective.

"We need to figure out Prince H.F.S.'s identity," Agatha replied quickly. "He's the true villain behind the giraffe's disappearance."

A sly expression crossed Dash's face. "Got anything in your memory drawers?" he asked. "Do you know any royals in any country with those initials?"

"I've got one idea," said Agatha. "But I'll need the EyeNet to confirm it."

"Sure, it should work fine up here. Just give me a second . . . it's a bit cramped," said Dash.

While he worked his hand under his seat belt and into his pocket to grab the device, Agatha continued to search her prodigious memory. "Ships that sail from Mombasa travel through

the Indian Ocean, often toward the Arabian Peninsula . . . The closest countries are Yemen and the Sultanate of Oman, which form the lower part of the peninsula. If memory serves, Yemen is a republic, and Oman is a monarchy." She paused when she noticed Dash looking confused. "Are you even listening to me?" she asked. "Monarchy? Prince?"

"Oh . . . right!" Dash grinned widely. "But what do I need to look up on the EyeNet?"

Agatha clasped her hands together, concentrating hard. "I may be mistaken, but I think the Sultanate of Oman uses honorific titles for the governors of each of its regions," she said. "Check to see if there's a regional prince with the initials H.F.S."

Dash didn't need to be told twice. He logged onto the Eye International archives and entered the new information. He was shocked to get a result immediately.

"Here it is!" he exclaimed in triumph. "Prince Husam Fadil Sayad!"

"Got him!" said Agatha with a smile, petting Watson's cool fur. He had climbed into her lap, taking refuge from the cold air at the bottom of the fuselage. "But what connection is there between Husam Fadil Sayad and our white giraffe?" the girl asked. "We'll need to prove there's a motive in order to catch him!"

Dash scanned through biographical files. A few minutes later, he showed Agatha the motive they needed to make their case.

"'A vast private zoo,'" she read. "'His palace garden, constructed in the middle of the desert, houses many unique specimens of mammals and reptiles, including some species that are nearly extinct in the wild.'" They looked at each other. It all fit together.

"But it's going to be hard to incriminate him." Dash sounded disheartened. "A lot of these

documents mention lawsuits brought against him by the World Wildlife Fund and Greenpeace, but they haven't succeeded in freeing the animals."

Agatha nodded. "Let's stick with one animal, for the moment," she suggested. "We need to focus on keeping Hwanka off that ferry and bringing him back to the Masai. We'll worry about the rest later!"

For the next few minutes, Dash concentrated on researching the *Bright Star*. It was a merchant vessel that shuttled back and forth weekly between Kenya and the Sultanate of Oman, transporting hundreds of shipping containers.

Agatha scrawled their discoveries in her notebook, tore out the page, and reached her arm across to the biplane's cockpit to show it to Chandler. It was the only way they could communicate, since the engine noise made it impossible to hear him.

The butler nodded, looking troubled. Then

he scrawled a reply and passed the page back. It read:

LOSING FUEL. MAY NEED TO MAKE EMERGENCY LANDING.

With all the problems they already faced, this was the last thing they needed!

Agatha leaned her head out, noting a small leak in the fuel tank that dispersed a fine mist of droplets into the air. Why hadn't anyone noticed this sooner?

They sat in stunned silence, holding their breath. Then, as the blue line of the coast appeared ahead, the biplane suddenly started to lose altitude. The wings trembled and waved. A sharp whistling filled their ears. The airplane began to tilt downward.

"Will we be able to land on the beach?" Dash looked terrified.

Agatha frantically searched the coastline, trying to find a stretch of empty sand for their landing. "If we come in too close, we'll hit those palm trees. If we go too far, we'll end up in the sea!" she replied. "Pass me the binoculars!"

After a quick scan, she picked out a wide stretch of treeless beach, which she pointed out to Chandler.

Tense minutes followed.

The biplane's engine cut out and only its wings kept them aloft. They felt a plunging, roller-coaster sensation, but Chandler's skilled maneuvers maintained the plane's balance. Their landing was very noisy as the wheels hit the beach, bouncing over the sand and zigzagging between deck chairs, beach umbrellas, and small tables.

When they finally came to a stop, the three Londoners staggered out of the plane, brushing sand from their clothes. Watson stared at a crowd

of stunned onlookers. Luckily, no one had been hurt. One tourist had filmed the whole thing on his smartphone.

The beachgoers who'd witnessed the skilled landing clapped loudly under the blinding sun.

Dash threw his arms up like a rock star, but Agatha pulled at his sleeve. "Let's go!" she said firmly. "There's no time to lose!"

"The docks are a long way away, Miss," observed the butler, squinting down the coast at the distant city of Mombasa.

"We'll take a motorboat!" exclaimed Agatha.

They sprinted toward the short pier, where there was a cluster of "beach boys"—young men who crowded the Mombasa beaches, offering to take tourists on boat trips. The trio approached one boy who ushered them onto his boat, and within moments, they were speeding across the calm turquoise sea.

It was already seven o'clock and their hopes were stretching thin. Agatha and Dash stood at the bow, checking the coastline. Chandler looked on as the boy drove the boat at top speed.

When they reached the docks, they got a nasty surprise.

"The *Bright Star* has left its moorings!" cried Dash. "We've lost our giraffe for good!"

"No, we haven't," said Agatha firmly. "There's still a chance."

The others stared at her, bewildered.

"We'll catch the ferry!" she said.

*T*he huge ferry moved at snail's pace, so the speedboat caught up with it before it reached international waters. The detectives pulled up alongside its thirty-foot-high side. How could they possibly get up onto a deck that high?

"We need a long rope and a grappling hook!" Dash shouted, turning to Chandler.

"Well, I don't happen to have one in my pocket," the butler said dryly.

"Then we need a flare!" Dash insisted.

Chandler rummaged through the boat's toolbox, then threw his arms up in surrender.

"I have an idea," Agatha added, nervously

biting her lip. "But we'll need to be quick!"

She directed their guide to speed up and position the boat directly in front of the ferry, but to maintain a safe distance. Then she asked Dash to place a phone call via the EyeNet.

"Will they take the bait?" her cousin asked.

"Guaranteed!" Agatha smiled. She hoped she was right.

When the smaller boat moved into the *Bright Star*'s path, the ferry's alarm horn sounded.

TUUUUUUUUUM!

Some sailors leaned over the ship's bow, signaling them to get out of the way. They called out to others working on board, but their cries were scattered by the sea breeze and the sound of the enormous engine.

TUUUUUUUUUM!

Agatha recognized John McDuff's mustachioed figure on board. Even though it was nowhere near teatime, he was standing on

deck with a steaming cup, calmly munching a digestive biscuit. "It's him!" she yelled to her cousin.

The young detective used his EyeNet to call the *Bright Star*'s captain on his marine radio. Dash explained that the elderly trophy hunter had forgotten to bring his heart medication and was in grave danger.

TUUUUUUUUM!

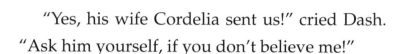

"Yes, his wife Cordelia sent us!" cried Dash. "Ask him yourself, if you don't believe me!"

A tense minute passed as McDuff was joined by a ship's officer. They exchanged words. The hunter squinted curiously at the small boat, where Chandler held the pill bottle aloft in his best English butler posture. McDuff nodded his assent to the officer, who turned his gaze to the navigation cabin and spoke into a radio.

The captain offered no further communication with Dash, but the *Bright Star*'s engines stopped churning and a rope ladder was thrown over the side. Agatha and her companions climbed up on deck and were immediately surrounded by half the crew. The young beach boy turned his skiff and sped back to the dock.

"What a reckless thing to do!" the captain raged at the group. "Couldn't you have contacted us before we left the dock?"

John McDuff stepped forward, his hunting

cap in his hands. "These fine English people are friends," he said in a gentlemanly tone. "If they've angered you, I shall accept full responsibility."

"Fine, McDuff," replied the captain. "Get it over with, then. We need to keep going."

"I'm afraid we'll have to ask you to return to port," Dash said, grinning strangely.

Agatha elbowed him in the ribs to make him stop smiling. As the crew returned to their posts, she gave the pill bottle to John McDuff, along with a sharp rebuke. "Your wife is very angry. You promised her you wouldn't go on any more dangerous hunts!"

"I know, I know. I've resisted the temptation for years," he apologized. "But I received such an enticing request that I couldn't resist the call of adventure."

"We know you were employed by the prince," said Dash. "Where is the white giraffe?"

The gentleman looked as if he could be

knocked over with a feather. "But how on earth . . . ?" he stammered. "Did Cordelia . . . ?"

"We've brought you your heart medication," Agatha interrupted. "And in exchange we want you to free an endangered and sacred animal!"

McDuff looked confused. Agatha outlined their meeting with the Masai *oloibon* and all that had happened until their pursuit of the ferry. When she finished, McDuff leaned against the railing, visibly shaken. "We must rectify this embarrassing situation at once," he declared solemnly.

He summoned his three assistants, spoke a few sentences in Swahili, and sent them to take a message to the captain. Then he led the group down to the hold, where they were keeping Hwanka. As they descended belowdecks, the elderly man smoothed his handlebar mustache and said, "I only accepted the job on the condition that the white giraffe would be transported safely

and no one would harm the fine fellow!"

Agatha was happy to hear it. She suspected that John McDuff was a good-hearted person underneath all his bluster. His only weakness was an unbridled passion for hunting big game, a remnant of the days before it was illegal. Now, however, he seemed to regret his actions, particularly because of the distress it had caused the Masai tribe.

"Here is our lovely friend," he said, eyes full of joy. "He's a capital fellow." They'd set up an enormous cage in the hold; the giraffe had room to move around, drink from a large dish, and eat acacia leaves dangling from a tall tree-like stake.

Agatha and Dash moved closer to pet Hwanka's astonishing milk-white coat, and told McDuff they would need to release him in the Masai Mara as soon as possible. He informed them that the ferry was already heading back to Mombasa.

Double Rescue

With deep sighs of relief and exhaustion, Agatha, Dash, and Chandler leaned against Hwanka's cage, while McDuff went to phone his wife and assure her that he had survived.

It was over!

"Why didn't you ask me to contact the ferry before it set sail?" Dash asked Agatha. "We could have saved ourselves all this trouble!"

"Too risky. If they'd known in advance, they would have had time to change plans," Agatha explained.

Just then, the horn sounded and they realized that the *Bright Star* had arrived at Mombasa's port. McDuff led them back up on deck, where they stood to admire the enchanting harbor, surrounded by white sandy beaches and crystalline waters. Before docking, they tried to reach Haida on her cell phone. As often happened in Kenya, the call wouldn't connect, and they had to send a text message with their happy news.

"I caused this frightful mess, so now I must set it to rights," declared McDuff as the giraffe's cage was winched off the boat and lowered safely back onto the dock. "We shall head back to the Masai Mara, and within days, young Hwanka will rejoin his herd."

"And who's going to tell Prince Husam Fadil Sayad?" asked Dash.

"That's my job as well!" the elderly hunter promised, thumping his chest.

Suddenly, Patrick Lemonde burst onto the scene pointing a rifle. "That's not the way it's going to go, McDuff!" he cried menacingly.

The sailors scattered, leaving only the trio of Londoners and the elderly hunter to face the gun-toting anthropologist.

Patrick Lemonde began to speak. "That giraffe is going right back on the boat," he ordered. "He's worth millions of dollars and I'm not about to lose it because this old man got sentimental!"

"But who are you?" asked McDuff, flabbergasted.

Agatha clenched her fist. "I suspected that you were the one who told the prince about the white giraffe. You betrayed the Masai tribe and your colleague, Annette, and you tried to sabotage our operation," she said in one long breath. "That's right, isn't it, Patrick?"

"You guessed it, brat." He sneered.

"I realized someone had loosened the Land Rover's tailgate before the rain started," Agatha continued. "Then, in the confusion, you planted a nail in the Land Rover's tire, and later on, you drilled a hole in the biplane's fuel tank."

"Excellent summary," Patrick said with contempt. "But you're forgetting one thing!"

"What's that?" asked the girl.

"Don't you recognize this? It's Haida's rifle. I've tied her up inside the Land Rover," he growled. "You wouldn't want your brave cousin to meet a nasty end, would you?"

Agatha expected Chandler, who still had a boxer's powerful right hook, to knock the man flat, but it was someone else who put an end to Lemonde's threats.

Hwanka silently lowered his long neck and plucked the gun from the man's hands with his rough tongue. The second he was disarmed,

Patrick was immobilized in the butler's iron grip.

"How does that feel?" Dash taunted him. "You'll get your own cage soon enough."

The sailors had summoned the harbor police, and Patrick Lemonde accepted defeat. He told them where he had parked the Land Rover, and two of the officers went to free Haida.

Meanwhile, Agatha asked everyone to listen as Lemonde explained his motives.

"When I discovered that Prince Husam Fadil Sayad collected rare animals," he began, "I couldn't resist temptation. He's a billionaire, and I asked for a pile of money in exchange for a live white giraffe. I used McDuff as an intermediary without revealing my identity. I knew he'd respond to a hunting challenge, so I took advantage of his weakness—"

"I didn't do it for the money," the hunter interrupted indignantly.

Agatha shushed him. "Go on," she urged Lemonde.

"You see, when McDuff captured Hwanka, I let Annette convince the *oloibon* to call Eye International to solve the investigation, so she wouldn't suspect I was in on it. And I steered her to a London office to buy us some time. I never imagined I'd end up with these young busybodies getting in my way!"

Agatha gave a sly smile. "It was a grave mistake to underestimate the Agent DM14's mastermind skills," she said happily. "Case closed, everyone!"

EPILOGUE

Mystery Solved...

$\mathcal{T}$hree days later, Hwanka was released back into the wild from which he'd been stolen. Before rejoining his herd, the white giraffe turned toward the small group of well-wishers and bobbed his head as if to thank them.

John McDuff and his wife, Cordelia, stood by hand-in-hand, visibly moved as they watched the giraffe walk away with halting grace until he disappeared among the acacias.

"It's up to you, now, young chap!" the elderly hunter exclaimed with pride. "Go back to the river and your Masai friends and we'll trust that everything will right itself!"

And so it did.

Agatha and her friends crossed the open savanna on foot under Haida's safe guidance. They'd already given Annette Vaudeville the news, and the anthropologist had been furious, not just because of the heinous crime leading to Patrick Lemonde's arrest, but because her colleague had fooled her for so long and she hadn't suspected at all. But peace in the tribe was the most important thing, so she decided to tell the tribal elders simply that Hwanka had gotten lost in the dangerous highlands and had now safely returned.

It was the best solution for everybody.

The *oloibon* decided to invite the foreigners who'd found the white giraffe to their village, and organized a big celebration.

Feeling serene, the group continued to walk across the majestic wild grasslands of Africa in silence.

"Do you know the meaning of the word *safari*, dear cousin?" Agatha asked Dash, winking at Haida.

"What kind of question is that? Piece of cake!" snorted Dash. "Everyone knows it means hunting big game with a gun or a camera!"

"Nope!" replied Agatha.

"Ah . . ." Dash paused. "Well then . . . maybe it refers to observing wild animals in their native habitat?"

"Wrong again!" Agatha retorted with a smile. "Haida, do you want to tell him?"

Their cousin nodded solemnly, stopping in the middle of the tall grass and gesturing widely with her arms. "*Safari* means 'journey,'" she said in a reverent whisper. "A journey without limits or destination. A journey that lasts a lifetime and beyond."

These heartfelt, profound words filled everyone with a sense of great peace, as though

they were connected to all of the great mysteries of the universe.

Agatha started walking again. "And now let's go celebrate!" she said happily.

It was another hour before they finally spied the remote village. It was arranged in a circle, with a wall of sharp branches and thorny shrubs as protection. There was a ring of huts inside, and an enclosure at the center for goats, long-horned cattle, and oxen, the herdsmen's pride.

Being invited inside the gates of this deeply traditional community was an honor they'd never forget.

It was rumored that the white giraffe had already visited the river, spreading good fortune of all sorts, and the Masai warriors who had looked so stern with their spears now greeted the group with friendly smiles.

Annette told them the whole village was ready to celebrate their hard work. There was

only one thing left to do before the festivities could begin . . .

The three Londoners and Haida were taken separately into low, straw-roofed huts, their wooden frames walled with woven dried grasses and mud. When they emerged, they exchanged glances. They could almost have been mistaken for members of the tribe in their red tunics and

adornments of silver and beads. The village elders gathered around their guests and began to speak in their language.

"What are they saying?" Dash whispered.

"They're giving each of you a Masai name," Annette replied. The anthropologist smiled wryly every time the *oloibon* announced a new nickname. She translated for the guests. "Agatha, they're calling you 'Yellow Butterfly,'" she said with a nod. "Haida is 'Kind Panther,' and for Chandler they've chosen 'Thoughtful Hippopotamus.'"

"HAHAHAHAHA!" Dash doubled over with laughter. "Thoughtful Hippopotamus!"

Silence fell over the village as everyone stared at the young detective, affronted. The elders decided to change the name they had given him as a punishment.

"What?" Dash grumbled as they were escorted to the large hut where the feast would

take place. "I don't want to be 'Crazy Baboon'! I don't deserve it!"

Chandler simply raised an eyebrow in reply. Agatha sat on a straw mat, thanking the elders respectfully. "Dash, I recommend that you don't make another scene, and politely accept what they've chosen to call you," she whispered. "I promise I won't write it down."

"You'd better not! I'll have perfect manners from now on," he promised as he reached both hands for the bowl he had been offered. It looked like it was full of chocolate milk and he gulped it down in one swallow. The rich, savory taste reminded him of something he couldn't quite place. Then he felt a sudden burst of energy shoot through every part of his skinny frame.

Just at that moment, his EyeNet beeped with a message from his professor, congratulating Agent DM14 on another successful mission.

Dash was thrilled. He quickly finished his

meal, then ran out to dance with the Masai. He was bounding around like a gazelle, jumping higher each time, beside himself with joy. Around him, the warriors clapped their hands, laughing louder than ever at his antics.

"I'm the village celebrity!" shouted Dash, turning to his companions as they came to join him in the clearing of hard-packed red earth. "I'm dancing with the stars!"

Agatha smiled. She whispered to Haida and Chandler, "If Dash only knew what he just drank, he wouldn't be so quick to gloat!"

"Why? What was in the bowl, Miss?" Chandler asked.

"A concoction of goat milk and ox blood," Agatha laughed. "It's very nutritious, but you know how finicky Dash is!"

"I'm not gonna tell him," said Haida, laughing.

Dash waved his arms, urging Yellow Butterfly, Kind Panther, and Thoughtful Hippopotamus to join the circle of dancers. He continued to spin and jump until late in the night, when bonfires were lit and the savanna echoed with the timeless rhythms of African drumming.

For a long time after that night, everyone in the village told stories of Crazy Baboon, the funny, energetic, terrible dancer who dreamed of becoming the greatest detective in the whole world.

Agatha

Girl of Mystery

Agatha's Next Mystery:
The Hollywood Intrigue

The Investigation Begins...

*D*ashiell Mistery was fried. While all his friends were hanging out in London parks, enjoying their freedom from school, his summer vacation had not even begun. In fact, Dash was starting to think this might be the year when he wouldn't get any vacation at all. Ever since he had enrolled at the prestigious Eye International Detective Academy, he'd been sent all over the world on daredevil investigations.

This time, though, his exhaustion was not the result of a top secret mission. A lanky, lazy teenage boy who loved staying up late, Dash didn't have a clue what he was getting himself into when he signed up for an intensive summer martial-arts class offered by his school.

On this Saturday morning, his muscles and bones ached. Dash dragged his stiff legs out of bed, microwaved three chocolate-chip pancakes, and shoveled them into his mouth. Then he hoisted his backpack onto his shoulder and left his mom's penthouse apartment at Baker Palace. It was still early, and the city sidewalks were almost deserted. Dash trudged to the nearest Underground station and sprawled across two empty seats on the short ride to his destination.

The martial-arts dojo was right in the center of London, neatly hidden among tall brick buildings. Dash knocked on a large wooden door decorated with Japanese calligraphy. An ancient Japanese man swung it open. He had white hair and a drooping mustache, and was wrapped in a monk's cloak.

"Good morning, Lazy Squirrel," Sensei Miyazaki greeted Dash with a knowing smile. "Are you ready for your training?"

Dash grunted. Snarling, he crossed the Zen garden to the wooden pagoda where classes were held. Lazy Squirrel? What a ridiculous name! Not to mention the cheesy metaphors his teacher was always using to explain martial-arts fundamentals. Dash had signed up for the class because he'd always dreamed of inflicting lightning-fast strikes like Bruce Lee, coolly dodging bad guys like James Bond, and launching himself into acrobatic moves like the heroes of *The Matrix*. But through all the weeks of exercise, he hadn't learned anything even close to that cool.

While Sensei Miyazaki waited under the pagoda with his arms folded, Dash pulled his white uniform *gi* from his backpack, slowly put it on, and walked barefoot to a large stone in the middle of the garden.

"Ready when you are, Professor . . . um, Sensei," he mumbled. "Same deal, right? I have to . . . what, free my monkey mind from negative thoughts?"

"Black clouds always bring on a storm," the

old monk intoned. Then he rotated his palms in the air, closed his eyes, and tilted his chin upward. "Now breathe . . . breathe . . . ," he said.

"How long do I have to . . . um . . . breathe, breathe?" Dash asked, gulping oxygen.

"Until your skies are calm, Lazy Squirrel," the teacher replied. Then he disappeared inside the pagoda.

The young detective spent the next few hours sitting cross-legged on the stone. Zen meditation wasn't really his thing; instead of calming him down, a million questions careened through his head. Was Sensei Miyazaki really an Eye International agent? And if so, why wasn't he teaching Dash how to fight bad guys, defend himself with his bare hands, and do cool flying kicks? And—the most pressing question of all—when was lunch?

He didn't realize he had dozed off until a sudden snap of fingers woke him at noon.

"I didn't do it!" Dash jolted awake. "What's up?"

The elderly monk stood in front of him, calmly crunching a sesame cracker. "Time for your first test of the day," he announced. "This ancient technique is called the Twisted Eel."

"What?" Dash protested, standing abruptly. "Don't I get a lunch break?"

Sensei Miyazaki's mustache quivered in disappointment. "This isn't a restaurant, Lazy Squirrel," he said stiffly. "You're here to learn"— *crunch, crunch*—"not to gorge yourself."

Dash's stomach was growling, but he obeyed. The only way to get out of here as soon as possible was to satisfy his teacher's demands. But when Dash stepped around the corner of the pagoda, he was stunned. The whole space was filled with a forest of ropes lashed to sturdy bamboo poles. The ropes were stretched at various heights and angles, tied close together like a giant web. "What is all this?" he asked, alarmed.

Miyazaki's lips stretched into a mocking grin. "To free yourself from your adversaries, you must learn to slip from their grasp like an eel," he replied, raising one finger. "Make your way to the far side without ever touching a rope . . . if you can!"

Dash cracked his knuckles, determined. He would prove his worth by passing this test without a hitch! He avoided the first rope by tilting his head sharply, then pivoted on his toes over the second. He flexed his thin shoulders backward and slid under the third as if doing the limbo. "Piece of cake!" he exclaimed, jumping over the next.

As he gloated, Dash heard a loud trill coming from the backpack he'd left near the meditation stone. Inside its front pocket was the precious multifunction device he used for school: a state-of-the-art high-tech gadget known as the EyeNet.

The insistent ringing could only mean one thing: He'd been assigned a new mission!

Momentarily distracted by that thought, Dash tripped over a rope. He pitched forward a few feet and landed, half-dangling from a dense tangle of ropes, facedown in the grass. With a mouthful of dirt, he didn't even say, "Ouch!"

"Are you hurt, Lazy Squirrel?" Miyazaki sounded concerned.

A hand shot out from the tangle of knots. "Sensei, please pass me my phone!" exclaimed Dash. Noting the monk's hesitation, he added in a whisper, "It's my EyeNet. Must be something urgent!"

When Miyazaki handed him the titanium device, Dash checked the message on-screen, and his eyes widened. Without realizing it, he managed to extricate himself from the ropes in a single smooth move.

"Hollywood . . . ?" he muttered, running a hand through his hair. "Are they out of their minds?"

Amazed at the skill with which his young student had freed himself, Sensei Miyazaki stood speechless as Dash took off like a flash. Before the teacher could even congratulate him, Dash had disappeared into the London streets.

Of course, Dash had rushed off to get help from his genius cousin, Agatha Mistery.

An Unforgettable Anniversary

Mistery House was a bright spot of color in an otherwise gray London suburb. Today, the lavender-roofed Victorian mansion had a sparkling air of celebration. In the luxuriant gardens, fountains gushed among blooming rhododendrons, while classical music spilled out from the house. It was just the right atmosphere to celebrate the anniversary of indefatigable jack-of-all-trades Chandler's twelfth year at Mistery House.

"Such a shame Mom and Dad got held up in Tasmania," said Agatha, casting a disappointed gaze at the impeccably set table, loaded with goodies. "It would have been perfect if they were here, too."

"They'll be home soon enough, Miss Agatha," replied the impassive butler as he settled into a chair. The former heavyweight boxer's bulk provoked a loud creak, but the chair held his weight. "I'm very grateful for all this attention," he added softly, his voice betraying emotion.

Agatha tapped the tip of her small, upturned nose with one finger, an unmistakable sign that she was pondering something. "Do you know what my parents are doing down there?" she asked, her eyes shining.

"I'm so sorry, Miss Agatha." Chandler shook his head gravely. "I have absolutely no idea."

"Before they left London, Mom mentioned they wanted to study a rare local species," said Agatha, passing him a silver platter of oysters. "Try to guess which one!"

"The famous Tasmanian devil?" the butler guessed. He swallowed a tasty lemon-and-parsley-sprinkled oyster in one gulp. Agatha had ordered all of his favorite foods for this anniversary lunch.

"The largest carnivorous marsupial in the world? No, too obvious!" Agatha laughed. "You won't believe it, but they're studying some slimy green frogs that live only in sulfurous jungle swamps . . ."

"Slimy frogs? Sulfurous swamps?" Chandler echoed. He lowered his gaze to the briny shellfish on the platter, suddenly losing his appetite. Struggling to maintain his usual calm, he asked, "What's so special about these frogs?"

Agatha pulled her leather-bound notebook from her back pocket. She always kept it with her in case she needed to record any detail of a topic that tickled her fancy. Like all members of the Mistery family, Agatha had chosen to pursue an unusual career. She wanted to be a world-famous mystery writer, and was always taking notes for her stories.

"I've consulted some of the scientific magazines in the library over the past few days," she explained, flicking through the pages. "It seems that this particular species has a gland that possesses miraculous medicinal properties."

"How extraordinary," Chandler said politely.

He was very familiar with his young mistress's talents: an incomparable memory, dazzling intuition, attention to detail, and many other qualities that made her a decidedly out-of-the-ordinary twelve-year-old girl.

"But what am I thinking? Our lovely lunch will get cold." Agatha excused herself, put her notebook away, and grabbed a seafood skewer. "You know what?" she said, beaming. "I'm glad to be celebrating this anniversary with you and our darling cat, Watson. You're the best friends anybody could have!"

"Aren't you forgetting somebody, Miss Agatha?"

Agatha looked amused. "You mean my dear cousin Dash?" she asked, twirling the skewer playfully. "I invited him, too, but he said it was a bad time. He's enrolled in some crazy martial-arts course and needs to practice all day. But I bet he'll drop in to say hello before the end of the day. He won't want to miss a slice of your—"

Agatha stopped in midsentence, covering her mouth with her hand. "Ooops . . . I'm such a loudmouth!" she said, blushing. "I nearly ruined the surprise!"

The butler raised an eyebrow, pretending that he knew nothing. That morning, he had spotted a five-layer Sacher torte on a platter in the pantry. The delicious Viennese chocolate-and-apricot-jam layer cake was his favorite dessert.

Agatha quickly changed the subject, and as soon as they'd finished their lunch, she asked Chandler to close his eyes and wait for her to bring his surprise gift to the table.

That was the moment when everything stopped being perfect.

"Watson!" Agatha cried in despair as she entered the pantry. "What have you done?"

Chandler turned off the opera CD they'd been playing and peeked through the partially open door. Attracted by the delicious aroma, the white Siberian cat had climbed on top of the cake, spreading whipped cream all over the counter. Now he was cleaning chocolate and apricot jam from his fur as though nothing had happened.

"Why couldn't you raid the leftover fish like a normal cat?" Agatha scolded. Grabbing a bar of soap, she turned on the sink and thrust the cat under running water. Watson yowled as water and bubbles flew everywhere. "You're such a bad boy!" Agatha told him, unable to suppress a smile. "Stop complaining—you need a good scrub."

As if bathing a furious cat wasn't chaotic enough, the doorbell rang. Chandler got up to check the security camera on the front gate and saw a police officer holding a figure in what looked like loose white pajamas. Watson leaped out of the sink and ran upstairs, leaving a trail of wet paw prints.

"It's the police," said Chandler.

To be continued . . .